HEIFER®
INTERNATIONAL

TOGETHER

Written by
Dimitrea Tokunbo

Illustrated by
Jennifer Gwynne Oliver

Scholastic Inc.
New York Toronto London Auckland Sydney
Mexico City New Delhi Hong Kong Buenos Aires

Library of Congress Cataloging-in-Publication Data
Tokunbo, Dimitrea.
Together / Dimitrea Tokunbo, Jennifer Gwynne Oliver.-- 1st ed.
p. cm.
"Cartwheel Books."
Summary: When the animals and the farmer work together, a great deal can be accomplished.
ISBN: 0-439-80323-3
[1. Cooperativeness--Fiction. 2. Farm life--Fiction. 3. Domestic animals--Fiction.
4. Animal sounds--Fiction. 5. Stories in rhyme.]   I. Oliver, Jennifer, ill. II. Title.
PZ8.3.T569Tog 2005   [E]--dc21   2005012455
10 9 8 7 6 5 4 3 2 1   06 07 08 09 10

Book design: Keirsten Geise
Printed in Singapore 46
This edition first printing, September 2006

For Maggie Stevaraglia

—D. T.

For my parents,

Karen Oliver and Dr. Wayne A. Oliver

— J. G. O.

"Cockadoodle doo!" the rooster crows.

He wakes up all his friends.

Giving to me, giving to you,

together there's a lot we can do.

"Moo, moo, moo," goes the COW.

She makes rich, creamy milk.

Giving to me, giving to you,

together there's a lot we can do.

"Cluck, cluck, cluck," the **chicken** says.

She gently lays an egg.

Giving to me, giving to you,

together there's a lot we can do.

The sheep bleats, "Baa, baa, baa."

She gives us warm, soft wool.

Giving to me, giving to you,

together there's a lot we can do.

"Bow wow-wow," barks the dog.

He protects and herds the sheep.

Giving to me, giving to you,

together there's a lot we can do.

The **mule** brays, "Hee-haw, hee-haw."

He moves a heavy load.

Giving to me, giving to you,

together there's a lot we can do.

"Tweedle-ee-dee," whistles the farmer.

He gathers fresh, sweet corn.

Giving to me, giving to you,

together there's a lot we can do.

The horse whinnies, "Neigh, neigh, neigh."

She pulls a cart of food.

Giving to me, giving to you,

together there's a lot we can do.

Giving to the world,

giving to you,

together there's a lot

we can do.

HEIFER®
INTERNATIONAL

Eight hundred million people around the world don't get enough to eat every day. With a problem this big, how can we make a difference?

Heifer International helps hungry families by giving them a very precious gift—the gift of a farm animal like a cow, chicken, or sheep. These animals provide food like milk, eggs, or cheese. With just this little bit of help, families that were once hungry will have plenty to eat.

The best part about these gifts is that families share them. Each family that receives an animal or training from Heifer agrees to pass on the gift of a baby animal to another hungry family.

Founded in 1944, Heifer International is a humanitarian assistance organization that works to end world hunger and protect the earth. Through livestock, training, and "passing on the gift," Heifer has helped seven million families in more than 125 countries improve their quality of life and move toward greater self-reliance. For more information, visit *www.heifer.org*.

READ TO FEED™

Afterword

by Jane Kaczmarek and Erik Per Sullivan

Lois on TV's *Malcolm in the Middle*

Together is a wonderful way for parents to introduce their children to a world beyond movies and television—a world where there are children just like them who, with the help of cows, goats, and chickens, are growing up stronger and healthier. It teaches them about where food comes from and how animals can make a difference in the lives of hungry families.

Dewey on TV's *Malcolm in the Middle*

There are so many hungry children in the world whose problems are much bigger than being the little brother. It's not easy to think about kids being hungry. When Jane, my TV mom, introduced me to Heifer International, I learned that there are millions of people who don't have enough to eat. But I also learned that there is a lot of hope—that a gift of a cow, goat, or chicken can make all the difference. *Together* makes the world of these farm animals come alive and teaches a very valuable lesson—that when we work together, we can accomplish anything.